TO OLIVER

You are the GREATEST!

Love from

....

Oliver is **THOUGHTFUL**,
And **HUGS** like a bear.
When you need somebody,
He'll always be there.

The FUNNIEST monkey you'll find at the zoo ...

Oliver will bring out the giggles in you!

A CURIOUS bunny,
Oliver wants to know
"Where did this come from?"
And, "How long ago?"

EGYPTIAN MUMMY

BRITAIN'S COOLEST MUSEUM

NO HUGGING
THE EXHIBITS

He's bananas for apples
And peachy for grapes ...

Oliver loves EATING
His food in all SHAPES!

When facing his fears,
He might find things
frightful ...

Then out ROARS
a lion,
So BRAVE and
delightful.

And even when things get
A little bit hairy,
Oliver just laughs,
"This isn't so scary."

This wise little owl's
Remarkably CLEVER,
He finds his way through
Almost any endeavour.

Oliver LOVES numbers,
And adds up with ease.
"I think I've enough
To buy five roses, please."

A real human rhino,
Our Oliver's STRONG –

BUS STOP

TIMETABLE

Tower of London
Brecon Beacons
Balmoral Castle
Titanic Belfast
Ring of Kerry

Nothing's too heavy,
Too large or too long.

He NAPS like a sloth
And can snooze anywhere.

Oliver dreams BIG
Going here, going there.

Oliver's so BUSY,
He beavers along ...
HARD-WORKING
and FOCUSED,

So what could go wrong?

(And sometimes when things
Don't quite go to plan...
Our Oliver tries
Just the best that he can.)

As SWEET as a kitten
And utterly CUTE,
Oliver's so LOVING
And GENEROUS to boot.

He's travelled all over,
From farms to fairs,
To show someone special
Just how much he cares.

So, there now you have it,
Oliver's the best.
So FRIENDLY and FUNNY
And BRAVE ... and the rest.

There's no one quite like him ...
It's *TOTALLY* true!
The GREATEST kid *ever*?
Well, Oliver, that's ...